GW00707614

THE FIGURE
IN THE DISTANCE

Otto de Kat

THE FIGURE
IN THE DISTANCE

Translated from the Dutch by
Arnold and Erica Pomerans

THE HARVILL PRESS
LONDON

First published with the title *Man in de Verte* by
Uitgeverij G.A. van Oorschot, The Netherlands, 1998

First published in Great Britain in 2002 by
The Harvill Press
2 Aztec Row, Berners Road
London N1 0PW

www.harvill.com

1 3 5 7 9 8 6 4 2

© Otto de Kat, 1998
English translation © Arnold and Erica Pomerans, 2002

Otto de Kat asserts the moral right to be
identified as the author of this work

A CIP catalogue record is available
from the British Library

ISBN 1 86046 882 9

Designed and typeset in Sabon
at Libanus Press, Marlborough, Wiltshire

Printed and bound in Great Britain by
Biddles Ltd, Guildford and King's Lynn

THE FIGURE
IN THE DISTANCE

THE ALGONQUIN LAY IN NEW YORK LIKE A SMALL island. "The names of towns and small islands are feminine," sprang into his mind as he drew the comparison, a rule from the book of Latin grammar resurfacing after many years. Over and over again his father had gone through the book with him. Hours spent face to face, weeks of testing, and all that had stayed with him was a couple of exceptions.

He was sitting in the lobby of the hotel when a woman, almost out of breath, pushed the heavy curtains in front of the swing door aside. From behind a newspaper he had picked up, he watched her looking around. He was struck by the beauty of her face. The man at the table next to his tried to attract her attention, murmuring a name. She approached him, embraced him and stood by his side for a moment. Then he heard her say in a halting voice, "I couldn't bear it any more, you were so shy. I've run the last few blocks."

It was not just towns and small islands that were feminine.

I

He could touch them, they were standing so close. The edge of his paper brushed against her coat. The man stroked her cheek, took the bag from her hand and beckoned a waiter. The young woman leant her soaking umbrella against a chair. It was snowing outside. Furtively, under cover of his paper, he examined her face. Its unaffected beauty was radiant, open and without flaws. The contrast with his father's face hit him hard. That face had been a mass of blemishes, the consequence of a skin disease with ever-changing symptoms. He had lost count of the times he had visited his father in hospital and of how many doctors he had seen standing beside his bed. Then there had been that comic episode with the hypnotist who had shambled up the staircase every week. His father used to spirit the man away, disappearing with him into a small room where presumably he went through the rituals in silence. Fifteen minutes later, relieved and slightly abashed, he would shut the door behind the worker of magic.

"May I have some tea, please?"

The staff was unable to oblige. At five in the afternoon, the Algonquin was full of people ordering long drinks. Tea was not one of these. He asked for a Perrier and fell silent again. From the first moment he had stepped into the lobby, he had felt at home here. The hotel resembled a book left open at a page that would never be turned. There was dark panelling everywhere, walnut chairs with high backs, and the kind of sofas that were fashionable before the war. Worn telephones and lamps with faded shades were positioned in small alcoves. By the window onto West 44th Street, a man sold newspapers from teak racks, as well as journals and books that were displayed in antique cases. You could reserve theatre tickets with him, too – Broadway, off-Broadway, off-off-Broadway, sounds he knew but did not understand, signals from a sophisticated, elusive world.

"Where are we going tonight?"

The young woman's voice sounded challenging rather than curious. "'*Equus*,'" his unknown neighbour answered without a moment's hesitation. *Equus*, Latin for horse, a word so familiar that it stung him. He had seen the poster. It was the most popular play of the season. He had no idea what it was about, nor any wish to know.

He rarely went to the theatre. He could not now recapture the tremendous thrill he used to feel when he himself had acted in school plays.

He had been Haemon in Sophocles' *Antigone*, a play typical of the Dutch gymnasium, the grammar school. Haemon, son of an all-powerful father, is the lover of a high-minded woman. Drama piled upon drama; death, curses, love and madness abound. His lines were particularly bombastic, but he had juggled them as if they were his own. He had one pivotal scene, the confrontation with his father Creon. They stood face to face, he and Creon, an 18-year-old made up to look like a man of 50. He, Haemon, must and would rescue Antigone. He must and

3

would convince his father that their lives would be lost if Antigone were killed. He hectored, he pleaded, he accused. The pathos gone from the text, his voice never wavered; time stopped as they stood there, riveted together. He saw how tears welled up in his adversary's eyes, how the paint under his eyelashes melted. The auditorium lay like a dark silence beyond the lights, a vacuum. His own father was sitting somewhere in the audience, invisible, his ears bandaged after an operation.

The performance had taken place in the Palace, a splendid euphemism for a makeshift structure from the '50s. But the stage was large, the backstage full of drops and ropes and iron weights. Life would never again have the same vastness as it had on those bare boards. When his father climbed the steps behind the stage after the performance, he felt his throat tighten; he struggled not to break down. From that moment on, everything seemed less important. He had been Haemon, and acted with an unaccustomed freedom, with words that, though not his own, seemed somehow familiar. He had participated in a drama of love and fate and death. A source of amusement, no doubt, for the parents watching their children bite off more than they could chew from an antiquity beyond their comprehension. And yet, no experience would ever have the same intensity again, not the birth of his children or the death of his father. An unbridgeable gulf seemed to have opened between him and even these experiences. Meanwhile twenty years lay between the Palace with its

4

sloping dance floor and the Dixieland jazz band playing on the edge of the stage, and the Algonquin Hotel where Steve Ross, "the best bar pianist in town", was singing the blues at the piano. If he had to choose, he would choose the Palace, *Antigone*, his father. He would not admit that this was a hankering after his youth. Never again and nowhere else had he lived with such unbounded emotion, never had he been so unbearably happy.

During the days before the performance the temperature had fallen to zero. The basement where they rehearsed was ice cold, and when they loaded the scenery into cars, a white vapour had wreathed them. Their concentration on *Antigone* had been as unrelenting as the frost. School had ceased to exist, teachers and homework were dismissed from their minds. They had doubted if the world would ever know such brilliant acting again. But then again, it had been no act; they themselves were being banished, killed and crowned.

He walked with his father through the wings to the dressing room, the tension of the performance still spinning round in him. In the mirrors he caught a glimpse of his father's bandages.

"Shall we take a trip tomorrow? The Alblasserwaard is frozen."

He pointed at the mirror. "Will your ears be all right?"

"We'll leave at eight."

———

They had parked the car at Kinderdijk. It was bitterly cold. The sun emerged slowly through the mist and they watched the sky turn blue high above them. They were three, his brother, his father and himself. They were all good skaters, his father the expert with the longest strokes. "Glide as far as you can, let the skates do the work." His brother and he copied their father. Their code was: no steel racing skates, wooden skates only. If it got really cold, a couple of newspapers under the sweater, but never a jacket. Gloves only when essential.

They walked down the dyke to the canal, fastened their straps and moved away from the edge. Hard-frozen reeds along the banks forced them to the centre of the almost black ice. They formed a line, his brother in front, followed by his father, then him. Every quarter of an hour each would move up a place. Nothing was said, the rhythm was automatic. In fact, their speed took him by surprise. Their strokes followed one another effortlessly as they skimmed across the ice. They passed one village after the other, Streefkerk, Groot-Ammers, Ottoland, Brandwijk, now and then braking for ice sweepers or small strips of land they had to cross.

The sun felt warmer then, the last pockets of mist gone, the temperature just below freezing. The skaters coming towards them sometimes stopped to watch them. Disciplined and impassioned, they skated with a strange pride, unimpeded by anyone else, unimpeded by rules and regulations. He kept his eye on his father's bent-over back, on the hands clasped together. He had but one aim: to keep up with him. They were strung out along the ice. Low across the country-side were towers, farms, windmills, the Alblasserwaard lying exposed and unguarded as far as the eye could see. His awareness became focused and more profound. In the crystal-clear light he concentrated on his father. This was how he really was, this was how he would always remem-ber him. Not as the man in hospital, not as the man with the pharmacists' insurance policy, the ointments, the ever-changing diets. This was his father, the skater in front of him with his elegant, gliding stride, his refined movements. He could have seized his hands if he had wanted to, their speed being such that the rhythm would not have faltered. But the proximity was physical enough.

However powerful his outburst of emotion and yearning had been on the Palace stage the night before, he realised that the ice-skating excursion now claimed his entire attention. Had his father appreciated what Antigone and Haemon and Creon meant to him? – was that why he had brought him to a place where there was nothing but space?

They skated for hours, taking a rest now and then, until late into the afternoon. The sun set, and in the still air they never noticed how the anthracite-grey sky darkened over them, promising snow. Back in Kinderdijk, they untied their skates and walked along the dyke with light steps, feeling out of their element. All at once it began to snow. It was almost dark, and the snowflakes came down verti-cally. They said nothing, softly stamped their feet, and in the entire god-forsaken Alblasserwaard there were no three people more exultant than they.

———

"*Equus*": the poster was everywhere, on Fifth Avenue, on Broadway, in bookstores and trendy restaurants. In the snow-covered streets of the Village and in the *New Yorker* offices where he spoke with an editor who had been engaged for a whole year on an article about Flemish literature. The *New Yorker* was the most snobbish journal in America; no-one read it, everyone quoted it. Attempting to penetrate this Valhalla, he found himself in a building that resembled an old warehouse. Glass cubicles along narrow aisles gave the impression that this was the kind of place where one might pick up a selection of bolts, nails, screws or other hardware. In fact, the man he had gone to see had looked not unlike a storeman, lacking only the overall coat. They very quickly became embroiled in a curious conversation. He expressed his surprise that some-one should have chosen to occupy himself with Flemish literature for a whole year. The storeman protested.

"In many respects, Flemish literature is far more interesting than Dutch. I've come to appreciate the difference between the anaemic prose of the Dutch and the exuberance of the Flemish. I realise, of course, that the Flemish do not write as well, but they are full of passion. Hardly anyone in Holland dares to write seriously. It's really as if they avoided earnestness and emotion like the plague. I think the Dutch are so scared of their own seriousness that they take refuge in irony, construction, experiment. They are afraid of their own language and have forgotten the real meaning of their words. The Flemish sometimes forget to write properly, but their work is inspired, it has a soul, it lives."

He did not say much in reply. He knew that the man was right, that he had misjudged him. He was no snob, and certainly no storeman – he proved himself to be a real lover of literature, Flemish himself in a manner of speaking.

Back in the hotel, the difference between the *New Yorker* and the Algonquin preoccupied him: the one bare and ascetic, the other snug and warm. With a strange persistence, he was always seeking out hotel lobbies, only to discover that he was really looking for bare offices.

Was he looking for something particular? He didn't think so. He listened to the conversation between the man and the young woman. She was perhaps ten years his junior, edgy, stylish, direct. He listened to her laughter, her quick replies, watched her movements. Now and then he would draw her to him with a look. The hotel setting was ideal for the lazy, formless desire she aroused. Formless, disembodied, with a wisp, a hint of eroticism. He was a newspaper away from her, the width of an umbrella, a coat. But the bandied words, the little jokes and pleasantries, threw his desires into disarray. The silence he needed never materialised.

He did not know whether it was her capricious reactions

or her youth, but he started to think of the girl who once dominated every minute of his day. It was a winter, two decades before. The first time he met her, he did little more than listen. Since she did all the talking, their encounter could scarcely be called a conversation. It was not that he was embarrassed; in general he got on well with girls. But she always found his pace too slow. Her wit was far sharper than anyone else's, and she radiated such magnetism that he often wished the ground would swallow him up. During their first talk, he sat facing her, a low table between them, she on a sofa and he on a dining-room chair. For obscure reasons she chose to make her presence felt through him. Perhaps she suspected that he was not altogether stupid, or maybe she had heard that he had the choice of any girl he fancied. She was a class above him at school, although she was not so much older. She spoke with an ease and fluency that surprised him – cutting, quicksilver, snide and flirtatious in turn. She had a whole repertoire of tall stories, interlacing them with numerous wisecracks. She imitated teachers, ran down her mother and pulled clown faces. And she never forgot that she was trying to impress the boy facing her.

Her expression was never still, and exhibited a mass of conflicting emotions, provocative in the extreme. She found it hard to curb her charm and it seemed as if she were determined to reveal her innermost feelings in record time. And she was never exhausted for a second.

The excitement he felt looking at her and listening to

her was not the usual pleasing sensation. It was the same excitement he had felt when he discovered that there were poets and writers, and that they described a world immeasurably vaster than his own, a world to which he had instinctively wanted to belong.

She was sixteen and at the height of her susceptibility. From the outset she gave him to understand that she wanted him close. But not closer than at arm's length. She believed that it was only without hands and legs that love remained undefiled. "The moment you touch me, I become a pariah," she kept repeating.

That winter he hung around her, wrote her letters and waited. She was more daring and sweet then than she ever was again. With unbridled energy she dragged him after her, and they went everywhere together. Churches, cafés, cinemas, striptease clubs, dance halls, he took her wherever she wanted to go. They ate together, went to parties, stayed in her parents' country house. He wore her scarf and inhaled her scent. She came close to him, held him tight, let him go. Calculation, innocence – she combined what she possessed in such ample measure: an enchanting talent to keep her life at the centre of his attention.

One afternoon he stood leaning against a wall in her room. She lived in a large house since her parents were rich, although she was not spoilt. He came to fetch her. Between the open windows she was looking at her face in a tall mirror, putting on make-up as he watched. He was at a loss how to react, finding it difficult to tolerate the blackening of her eyelashes. But she told him not to be silly and he was taken off guard when she suddenly flung her skirt up. The high spirits of her gesture misled him. She was wearing black silk knickers, and all she had done was hitch them up. Then she burst out laughing and flipped her skirt up once again for a final adjustment. It lasted only a few seconds, but he felt as if he'd been kicked in the stomach. He took a few steps forward, his chest aching horribly, and he turned her around. She gave him a questioning look, but before she could say anything he ran away.

———

Each table had a small brass bell for summoning a waiter. The soft tinkling from all sides did not disturb him. Every few minutes a smartly uniformed elevator operator would open the door of his elevator, then close the iron grill behind the guests with a dull thud. Without looking, the receptionist at the hotel desk reached for a key from one of the innumerable pigeonholes. Waiters strolled hither and thither carrying trays. A restaurant manager at a tall lectern wrote down reservations. The machinery was working, he thought, everything smoothly operating. The lobby was full of people talking with their mechanical mouths, their laughter, their blinking eyes. He hoped that the young woman next to him would say nothing more, that she would melt into the crowd, much as he would like to himself. The warmth, the subdued lighting, the cultured voices, plunged him into a state of passivity. He felt that

12

nothing he believed suited him. What had he sought at the Algonquin? The Algonquin meant quiescence, a dream, the past, or at best a vague *acte de présence*. Why was he here, why did he not relinquish the dream? He would not be able to bring his father back, no matter how he reshaped the past. New York, out there, confused him – it was an explosion of activity. He recognised the wild enthusiasm in it, the old idealism he had constructed over winters and summers past and which had never deserted him. But New York was a city without a beginning or an end, the connections lost within it. The old visions resurfaced; he would fight the good fight, battle against hunger, do good deeds. It was all a repudiation of reality, an ecstatic longing for immortality, for communion with his father. It was with concepts like these that, the night before, he tried to explain to Roy how this city confused him. Roy Dawson, his American friend, who had lived all over the world before returning to the land of his birth. Roy told him that, for his part, he was living a life without ambition. He had put his education, his experiences, his career aside, and was working in a small town on the coast, not far from the city. He worked at a maritime museum, looking after an old sailing ship. He polished the brass railings, scrubbed the decks, mended the sails. He loved the outdoor life, the waves, the wind, the sailing. He had shed all the worldly ambitions of his upbringing – he was sailing, and that was what he had always wanted to do.

From the dining room came the voice of Steve Ross

singing a Noël Coward song, that gentle cynic. He watched new guests walking into the hotel, stamping the snow off their feet.

And then it dawned on him that time was pressing.

THERE IS SOMETHING GRAND ABOUT WALKING downhill, he thought, making your way down the slopes towards the centre of the city, if you happened to live in a wood above it. Towards dusk every evening he would walk down the hill and every time he had the same enjoyable feeling. An invisible hand nudging him down the tracks, along the streets.

Zurich. At six o'clock without fail, he would leave his house to meet the sound of church bells. He could hear the thin chiming of the carillons far below him, the bells ringing the changes at different pitches, marked off by an occasional silence. He listened, hearing a strange melancholy.

He was on the way to the Altstadt, the centuries-old heart of the city. His house lay many hundreds of feet above it; no-one lived higher than he did. He could see all about him, the mountains on the other side, the lake, the crows coasting over the rooftops. As soon as the bells fell silent there was a lull in the urban rhythm. No disturbing noises to spoil his walk. For the first few hundred yards he met no-one. Occasionally a tram wobbled up towards the zoo, but there was never even a dog on the loose. If there were any sound at all then it was the thumping of his heart.

Eyes shut, he had pushed a pin into the map of Europe. He had to get away. Clothes, books, binoculars, a radio, a stack of writing paper, and a day later he had been in Switzerland. Zurich of all places. Somehow he felt at home around such shameless wealth.

He took rooms in an annexe of the Hotel Zürichberg, a huge building with terrace cafés, frequented by crowds of old people from the nearby rest homes. A temperance hotel established by women determined to keep Swiss men off the demon drink. As a result the place was full of ancients playing cards and eating cake. A charnel house, a pleasure ground straight out of Fellini. He had his breakfast there every morning, and no matter how early he was, the card players were already out in force. He took pleasure in their faces, the hum of their voices, the jauntiness of these candidates for death.

Thomas Mann had once stayed in this hotel, his first stop after being forced to flee Germany like a thief in the night. The writer Thomas Mann, whom his children called the Magician. Magician, illusionist, poseur, tricks up every sleeve, in short a writer.

It was hard to imagine a more violent contrast with his own father.

At ease, he strolled towards the night that came drifting out of the houses. Careful observation shows that night

16

does not fall, but emerges creeping from windows and doors. When the lights are switched on, the darkness slips outside. He had noticed this dozens of times.

"Let's hold onto the twilight for a moment," his father would often say when someone was about to turn on a light. His father's silhouette in a chair. One leg crossed over the other, cigarette smoke spiralling above him, his hand with the mysteriously-mangled nails on the round mahogany table. A still life, the hand lying beside two silver rings – the anklets of Indian princesses, so the story went – and next to them the leather-bound history of seventeenth century Amsterdam. His father, the anti-magician, was the magnet, the mirror, the resonance in his body.

Let's hold onto the twilight – he was surprised that the street lights had not yet come on. Swiss thrift, as like as not. It was the end of February, antechamber of spring. A blackbird was perching high up on the house he was passing, in dark outline against the embers of daylight. It sang, boldly, immoderately. Always the same song, year after year, and always beginning towards the end of February – his memory was annoyingly good at retaining such details. The sound took him criss-crossing back through his life.

———

"Catch," he called out to E. and tossed a jar half-full of jam at him. E. had plucked it out of the air and thrown it straight back, with a high cackling laugh. The windows of their room were wide open. E. and he stuck their heads out to see if there was anyone around to catch a jam jar. At about six o'clock, students would make for the refectories and clubs, but there was no sign of any of their friends.

E. sat down in the moth-eaten leather armchair he had found in a junk shop, and which they had hoisted with great difficulty into the room they shared. There were two desks side by side, a couple of upright chairs, some paintings and a pair of wobbly lamps, all that people who were frequently on the move would accumulate.

The hazy atmosphere of a warm June day hung all around. June 1967. The war in Israel was just over. E. and he were unreservedly on the side of the Israelis. They rejoiced when Israeli tanks reached the Suez Canal, and fervently hoped that Cairo would be attacked, or Damascus. Warfare at a distance was a pleasurable activity. Moshe Dayan was their hero, the one-eyed romantic with the appeal of the desert fox, shirt-sleeve diplomacy. E. was going to become a lawyer, or perhaps a diplomat, one of those negotiators who keeps the world's wheels turning. E. was his friend, the closest he was ever to have. Boyish, slight, with a keen gaze, a narrow face, a sense of humour and a feeling for music. It was not so much that they complemented each other – on the contrary. But they never felt a sense of emptiness when they were together. They never wearied of each other's company.

E. lit a cigarette. He had reached easily for a lighter in a special inside pocket of his jacket like a plantation owner, he fancied, and flicked it. They were not much above

18

twenty. Girls, literature, politics, studying as if there were no alternative: days without end, years without end.

"Where are we going tonight?"

"Garbo. 'Ninotchka'. Midnight at the Film Society."

"Is that the film where she finally laughs?"

"Yes, there's some feeble joke that gets told twice, but doesn't make her laugh. The man repeating the joke gets more and more angry until he falls off his chair and then she starts laughing, but so unnaturally that you feel like punching the director. Garbo should never have been allowed to laugh. I'm against it."

"Would she be able to catch a jam jar if you chucked it at her without warning?"

"She can't catch and she can't laugh, but she can do everything else. She is inhumanly beautiful, her voice is incomparable, and she acts . . ."

"All right, take it easy, calm down." E. lifted an eyebrow and pointed to the sofa opposite him.

"Lie down and relax, that's my advice," he said with the air of a psychiatrist, although psychiatrists were few and far between in their circles. They had an aversion to anything that smacked of therapy. And yet they were not unfeeling, far from it. Nostalgia, infatuation, desperate love for the wrong woman, writing verse, the theatre – they bombarded each other with feeling. Their friendship was to last seven years. Rich years.

A few months after the Six Day War they went to Israel. "To take in Dayan," they said – "to visit the hub of the world", "to witness a small miracle", "to see the desert that bloomed like a rose", they proclaimed, whether in context or not.

"This is where the Son of God walked on water."

"This is where Christ was baptised in the Jordan."

"This is where you can see the oldest church."

"This is where Begin's men cut the throats of hundreds of Palestinian men, women and children."

"What? What guide book is that in?"

They had walked through the hilly terrain between Jerusalem and Tel Aviv. Everywhere lay burnt-out wrecks, half-tracks, tanks.

"Christ!"

"Did not walk here."

"And afterwards that whole migration of peoples started. Hundreds of thousands of Palestinians fleeing over the border. I know that, the Israelis say nothing about it, and we act as if we didn't know. What a miserable business."

"What could be more beautiful than the Sea of Galilee?"

"Nothing so far."

"From which kibbutz shall we beg a morsel of bread tonight?"

"I can't face another kibbutz." E. started hobbling, putting on a limp. "Can I go home, please?"

The Prague Spring erupted. They lay with their ears glued to their radios. Never again would it sound the way it did that spring. Dubcek, Svoboda, Smrkovsky, Jan Palach – the resonance of all the names.

Paris began, permanent discussion, the imagination seizing power. They really believed that their world would continue to turn, they looked forward to living without constraint, to living gripping lives, if need be in permanent discussion, if need be democratised, if need be without a university degree. To live a thrilling life – or at least to read about it, hear about it, write about it. Several years later, E. was dead. Run over on a mountain pass in Afghanistan.

"Of all places."

———

The blackbird's song overhead stopped for a moment. He stood and watched as the bird swooped down.

Most lives are lived in a void. Everything is a constant replay of motions, a complete stalemate, a banging of the same head against the same door that refuses to open, that will never open. The same pictures, the same voices, the same words, the same instincts. A blackbird swooping away and singing the same indignant song on the next roof. Calling out to the world that you are there.

He was approaching the city itself. Music drifted across from the houses, trams sounded their bells at bends, cars hooted. Thomas Mann had arrived from Germany driving a large open car. With his wife Katja, Mann had rolled into the centre of town from Zürichberg in that open car. A mummy, a legend, a wizard, a maniac. Where he was now walking, Thomas Mann had once been driving. On the way to the Schauspielhaus, to the Kronenhalle restaurant, to a reading or a literary soirée in the Baur au Lac. He was the uncompromising, the brilliant, the unapproachable, the ambitious writer. With children who deferred to their father's talent, the shadows of a sun that shone day and night. With a son who killed himself.

In the meantime it had grown dark. He was on his way to a strange engagement. He was going to be made up and kitted out as a newspaper to celebrate Fassnacht, the Swiss carnival. His party would be waiting for him in the Kronenhalle, people he had met by chance and who had invited him to join them. He knew nothing about carnivals, and had never imagined he would be part of one. But in Zurich everything was fine as far as he was concerned, and no doubt he would survive.

It did not take him long to realise that Fassnacht was no small affair. Groups of musicians were crowding into the streets and squares from all directions. A parade of people in fancy dress, all eager for a good time.

The Kronenhalle was the most entertaining restaurant he knew. Every night the old proprietress would shuffle slowly past the tables to welcome her customers. The waiters indulged her, and when she had completed her rounds, she would drink half a bottle of champagne. She was ninety. The dining-room walls were covered from floor to ceiling with paintings by artists who had subsequently become famous and who had once been part of her clientèle. The authenticity of the paintings and the vulgarity of the customers dining lent the room an indefinable charm.

There was a Feininger – entitled "Manhattan" – which he had eaten under a few times. Skyscrapers in dark crayon. He kept thinking that it would fetch a great deal of money at auction. A beautiful thing, if sombre. His father had taught him to look at paintings, taking him along to viewing days in auction houses such as Mak's in Dordrecht.

In his mind's eye, it was always raining when they drove to Dordrecht on Saturday afternoons. He would be allowed to drive his father's swaying Citroën DS, more amphibious a vehicle than a normal automobile. A car as lovely as a Feininger. During the drive they seldom talked much. Sometimes his father ostentatiously pressed his hand against the dashboard to show that the braking had been too late for his liking. He would groan softly and give him a sidelong glance. And as they approached the long run-up to the bridge over the Noord, he would wonder if it was known that there was a 70 kilometres per hour speed limit on the bridge.

Viewing day at Mak's. They were both keen on the Romantics, nineteenth century Dutch picture postcards, and on painters of the eternal smallness of details. From his childhood, his father drew his attention to Schelfhout's wintry scenes, to Bosboom's church interiors, Vertin's streets, Verschuur's horses. He knew their names and their favourite subjects years before they came into fashion.

The naming of the painters was an invariable part of their days out. Before they reached the Visstraat the ritual exchange was over.

"It looks as if there's a fine Hoppenbrouwers on show," his father said.

"And a Springer."

"Springer's far too much of a chocolate-box painter for me."

"Isn't there anything by Ten Cate?"

The glossy catalogue crackled. His father still received the mailings, year in year out, simply because he had once bought a small painting at Mak's. And what he had snapped up then turned out much later to have a suspect signature.

"No. Just another Schelfhout as well as the whole Koekkoek family."

They tossed the names to and fro. It was like a conspiracy by amateurs to imitate the talk of experts. They only just avoided discussing the characteristic brush strokes of Spohler or Schouman, not for lack of trying but of knowledge. It was ritual, intimate.

He parked in the small yard next to the auction house. Holding on to his hat, his father walked beside him into the wind, his weather-beaten face wearing a good-natured expression. Dordrecht in the rain. The door of the auction house jammed a bit more every year. It was an ugly building with the appearance of a drill hall. But once inside, once past the woman who stuck tickets into hatbands and looked after the umbrellas, they were in their element.

They walked along the walls, past small lamps lighting up old cabinets, cut-glass vases, indeterminate objets d'art.

His father felt at home in this numbered jumble. He leafed through the catalogue, leant towards a nondescript man whom he had unerringly identified as an auctioneer. He had never seen his father walk up to another visitor and ask him what "that knick-knack over there" was likely to fetch. He himself preferred to buttonhole some innocent antiques buff, who would not answer but would shrug his shoulders to convey that he had no idea. He watched his father talking to the auctioneer, knowing that they were discussing prices, setting an upper limit, without the least risk that he would end up with the item. That was his father's way of keeping up with the auction world. He stopped in front of a display case holding silver brooches, clasps, spoons. Silver did not appeal to him much, jewellery still less. He looked up and saw that his father was no longer talking to the auctioneer. He had gone.

Oddly enough, his first thought was how tiresome it was to lose sight of his father just then. He wanted him within reach in case he saw something he liked. It was an almost imperceptible desire that had come to cling to him over the years, like coral to a reef. Before, when he had played in some tennis match, his father would stand somewhere in the background, generally where he could not see him from the court. When the applause rippled over him for a well-made stroke, he would wonder if his father had seen it, too. Once, during a tournament in another part of the country, he was beaten easily. No-one had known he was playing there. When the last ball was hit and he came off the court, he suddenly noticed someone in the distance leaning against a tree. A brief wave of a hat and his father turned and vanished from view.

He extricated himself from the small group of people around the showcase and started to outpace most of the other visitors past clocks and rugs, with the air of a child afraid of being left behind. The creaking stairs led up to a hall with less important pieces, curios, portfolios of bad drawings. Why the desperate need to see his father when he would be with him in the car again in an hour? It was an impulse not based on any decision – like someone picking something up that could easily have remained where it was, but feeling that order had been restored. He was about to go downstairs again when someone grasped his shoulder from behind.

"I was looking for you."

"Yes, I was looking for you, too. There's a Moerenhout in there. Someone's put it in, but it's not in the catalogue."

Moerenhout. At home they had a hunting scene by the artist – handed down from father to son for more than a century. "What could be finer than Moerenhout's 'Hunting with Falcons'," someone had written during the nineteenth century. They liked to repeat that whenever the smart set put their Schelfhouts on show. They had never seen one at Scheen's, that pompous connoisseur from The Hague.

Moerenhout had become a watchword. They uttered his name and, in a manner of speaking, heard the gas in the pipes and the electricity in the wires. Moerenhout – the word transported them into a state of euphoria, the air tingling all around them. He was enraptured by it.

They pushed their way through the small hall and stopped in front of the painting. They looked at it. And he was overcome by the sensation that his father was entering his body, settling permanently inside him. If only the looking could have lasted forever – he no longer heard the bustle all around him, everything had fallen into place. Nothing would ever again slip from his memory. His father would die, he would never see him again, and the Moerenhout would never again hang so beautifully. He was filled with nostalgia for a moment that had not yet passed. His father standing there, motionless, one hand resting on his shoulder. His eyes, his coat, the walls with the people walking past. If only the looking could have lasted forever.

The way back up the hill took longer. It was five o'clock in the morning, and little by little the commotion of the Fassnacht was dying down. There were still no trams running. From the Kronenhalle to the Zürichberg was an hour's climb. Left past the Kunsthaus, right past the Schauspielhaus, turn right at the University and then towards the zoo, the cemetery, the hotel.

Snow started to fall haltingly out of a dark sky. He could still hear half the night's music in his head. In his news-paper outfit, he walked into the restaurant and was drawn into a circle of friends as if he had belonged to it for years.

The place was packed, but not so full that again and again some new band or another couldn't join in. Guitars, trumpets, drums, even violins and clarinets. Every single person was dancing and singing. Where the girl sprung from he could not remember. He had been standing by a row of coats when, out of the blue, she put her arms around him and kissed him with abandon. Her mouth on his, he could even feel the softness of her tongue. The embrace was long. He was taken aback, but he found her total unfamiliarity peculiar and pleasing. She pressed herself against him, and the newspapers that poked out all round him became crumpled and flattened. "Le journal est un monsieur," he mumbled, but she didn't catch the joke. He ran his hand over her dark hair for a moment, saw that she had green eyes and was overwhelmed by her zest. At that point a group of musicians leading a long line of revellers came thundering through the hall. They plunged straight through the row of coats, straight through their embrace. She joined the surge, looked back and called, "Shall we dance?" He saw that she was much younger than he was, watched the freedom of her movements. She laughed, gave him one last wave and was gone.

He shivered. He had not anticipated snow. If there was a God, then it had to be a woman. The disappeared girl swam before his eyes. He wondered if she had mistaken him for someone else. She hadn't been drunk, she had done everything with deliberation and a lively infectiousness. From what superabundance had her gesture sprung?

Her anonymity was exciting. The capriciousness, the blast of wind, the overheard telephone call between unknown voices on a crossed line. Her history, which he did not know, the way she lived, what she thought and dreamed of. The abruptness of her approach, her animation, her lack of caution or fear.

His feet were slipping. The snow was getting deeper and deeper and the sugar-sprinkled street had turned treacherous. At first he felt wildly triumphant at such an embrace from the girl. Then came the wish to know who she was. But walking back uphill through the snow, he experienced only a happy sense of detachment. It was precisely her disappearance, her absurd wave of farewell, that he would not easily forget.

It kept on snowing. He passed the cemetery near the hotel. The gates were closed. James Joyce, one of the many wanderers who had lived in Zurich, was buried there, his grave marked by a small statue. A seated man, one leg crossed over the other.

E. used to sit like that, and he remembered that his father sat like that as well. His father, like E., had been cremated. No grave for him, but a dark moss-covered urn on a windy hill in Westerveld.

"Doesn't he look nice in there, sir?" the hospital attendant had asked when he had gone into the small vault to see his father one last time the evening before the cremation. He could not agree. The face he had looked down upon was calm but tired, with a sunken mouth. "Nice" was certainly not the word. Bowing, the undertaker shut the door carefully behind him, with the gesture of a man delivering eggs.

It was almost six when he opened the door of his room. He looked back. The small track he had made in the snow pleased him. He stood at the window, where the curtains were still open. The first light of morning glanced off the Rigi on the other side of the lake. He missed E. He missed his father. But every time their absence impinged upon him, the emptiness filled faster than it had come. He did not quite understand it, the ineffably beneficial effect of their loss. As if there were something to celebrate.

WHEN HE OPENED THE COLLEGE DOORS AND stepped inside, he was disorientated. The dark hall in which he found himself was cut off from the outside light. Cambridge, England. Hurriedly he reached into his pigeon-hole, then walked along the passage past the room with the snooker table. He could see the coloured balls glancing off one another, and two young men holding cues studying the state of play. Up the stairs, and then up more stairs, a short passage on the right, and he would have reached his room. He walked swiftly, clutching the two letters. He tore their envelopes even before he sat down. He could never settle down properly before half past ten, which was when he knew for certain whether there was any mail for him.

The cold clung to his coat. He had gone out right after breakfast. It was October, chilly with a thin veneer of sunlight. He passed the tall gates of Westminster College, where Protestant ministers were trained, leaving behind him the sound of the organ. Chanting, praying, reading out their lessons, with dogged persistence students and teachers climbed into their pews every morning to bless the day. Sometimes he would go and sit with them, listening but not joining in. That early in the morning he could scarcely bring himself to talk, let alone sing. He could not accustom himself to worship so soon after bacon and eggs.

He followed his usual route. The footpath alongside Queen's Road, strewn with wet leaves, through the small park that led to St John's. All the lawns looked lush for the time of year. There were flowers still, and the trees, although shedding their leaves, were not yet bare. A chapel bell struck nine in dry tones. Other bells chimed in from further away. Another hour and a half. The sun was glinting on the Cam, where ducks – their heads tucked under their feathers – were bobbing, and pigeons were pecking irritably at the soil. The surroundings lay on his retina like an abstract painting. He looked at them without great interest. He was taking the shortest route to the Copper Kettle, the café he visited every day. The small covered bridge at St John's carried him across the river to the heart of the College. The rounded cobblestones of the courts were slippery and the atmosphere felt as exacting and repressed as in an army barracks. He stood still as a procession of choristers came at the double across almost the entire width of the inner court. Boys attired in black and white trotted off to church at the most unlikely hours. Singing in the Anglican Church seemed to be a continuous business. He watched them disappearing one by one into the building. Involuntarily he tried to put himself in the place of the last boy. His desire to become lost in somebody else was becoming relentless. A form of immaturity. He wanted to lose himself or to conceal himself, and to that end he sought hiding places wherever he went. In people whom he met by chance, or saw on a bus, in an office, in a phone box. An inability to face his own life.

He left St John's, crossed the street diagonally and reached Trinity Street. The shops here were small and elegant, with windows sporting college scarves, umbrellas and books. Dark green and brown wooden fronts on which the proprietor's name was written in ornamental letters. Streets like mole runs, protected by a hedge of university buildings. He felt as if he was being gagged by an airtight rag. He pushed open the door of the Copper Kettle, and the voices as he passed sounded muffled. There was no-one there he knew, which meant he would not have to make conversation.

But the disintegration of his thoughts did not slacken. For weeks the space between his eardrums had been teeming with ever-smaller fragments – thoughts that buzzed senselessly, had nowhere to go and refused to disappear. He could not explain why so many details surfaced time and again. Surfacing was not really the right expression, in fact, since they rained down on him. A magic lantern gone berserk, producing an endless series of disconnected images. Images all from his past, it was true. There was some system in that the chaos invariably hinged on what had once been. He was living backwards. Hearing, seeing, feeling and thinking backwards.

He chose the red leather seat against the wall with a view of the street and of King's. He placed Nabokov's *Speak, Memory* on the small round table in front of him, stirred his coffee and waited. He left the book unopened; it lay there as his alibi, no more. He was in no mood for reading. The intrigues in Nabokov's life had not the least connection with his own. He often found the dozens of books he read quite meaningless. They were so many contrived tales, with the characters brushed on and then pasted in. Looking around, he saw a girl who bore a slight resemblance to K. – she had the same reserve that struck him as erotic. He sized up her breasts under her coat, almost routinely, quickly and with detached pleasure. Breasts lived a life of their own, unconnected to that of the woman that accompanied them.

Where might K. be right now, what would she be doing, what was she thinking, to whom was she talking, whom was she provoking with her cool, intriguing ways? Ever since he had watched her train leaving the bare Cambridge station, he had sunk into a state of restlessness he had never known before. Her pale face above her short fur coat, leaning out of the carriage window for a moment, and then nothing. The sense of falling apart he had felt after K.'s departure never left him, neither then nor now. He took a sip of his coffee and for no reason stirred it again. Past the window, just above the half-curtains hung

34

from a brass pole, faces hurried back and forth. They were no more than dark smudges in his line of vision.

He was afraid of missing out, afraid that life would pass him by without his ever having tackled it. And that he would lose the handful of people dear to him. There, in that English coffee shop, he realised that his reserves were drying up. Fear was something he had never really known. He had always run away from loss, had always filled the gaps with his formidable memory. But that no longer worked. The months in Cambridge were beginning to sap his easygoing self-confidence.

The night before, he had gone to the cinema with Roy. Emotions had ambushed him there – had physically shaken him. He had come out in a sweat, the darkened space having filled him with horrors. He had the greatest difficulty in remaining in his seat. Tears poured down his cheeks. An obsessive idea tightened around his neck like a noose: I must go to K., I must see her, I must touch her, she must say that she loves me, she must not be allowed to get away, I must go to K. It subsided, and he told Roy something about it when it was all over – Roy Dawson, the young American, who was also a visiting fellow in the College. They experienced an immediate rapport the moment they met, exchanging cracks at Protestant earnestness and concluding that the clank of billiard balls hitting one another was more edifying than the psalmody of a professorial parson. They preferred watching the Romanian cook baking them a cake in the kitchen to listening to a lecture on the Dead Sea Scrolls. They walked together through the town, or rode on Roy's motorbike at break-neck speed along the lanes that chopped the countryside around Cambridge into bits.

Imperceptibly his fixation on K. began to take concrete form, and Roy noticed. He lived with his wife Sabine outside the College in a cold and damp house in Mill Street, where they would sit talking all evening. Roy was a godsend in the English environment. He was something of a barbarian amidst all the venerators of books and theories. The centrifugal vanity of learning seeped deep into the lives of those who studied here. But unlike Roy he could appreciate the local snobbishness. The rites with which people celebrated their own excellence did not disgust him. On the contrary, he was attracted by the rhetoric of it all. Traditions were treated like a game; perhaps nowhere else in England did people laugh so much at the old humbug as in this town. He had been in the holy of holies at St John's, where the Fellows assembled, where the Masters presided, where cups of coffee and raised glasses of brandy tinkled before the great open fire. Glass in hand, he stood talking to a chemist. The polished dark panelling, murmured conversation all around him, the silver candle-sticks with the burning candles, nothing was allowed to spoil the impression that the world was being kept at bay. A little earlier, the chemist had quite probably been in his laboratory, participating in the filthiest of experiments, challenging the laws of the universe. Moments later he donned his black gown, pronounced the Latin grace, and leaned back in the College tradition. It was a sarcastic mockery. A masquerade. That was Cambridge: a place where you could hide yourself away without effort.

In those days he had come across an odd little book by a seventeenth-century scholar. The author proclaimed man's total inability to act and denied almost every form of knowledge; the "I" was the spectator at a play in which he had no part. "*Orbis terrae theatrum est* – all the world's a stage; and one thing I know for certain: I am not watching this drama by my own choice." He found a quotation from someone who referred to himself as a "vanishing speck in the terror of infinite space". They were the sayings of philosophers, extremely sober-minded and extremely poignant. They took him more by surprise than he cared to admit. The terror of infinite space. He had to put the book to one side and could think of nothing better to do than to place K.'s photograph beside it. She existed in that infinite space, and he did not want to lose her.

He envied Roy's lack of imagination. Roy adored the shine of his motorbike; he did what he knew best, following an unfailing instinct. In America, Roy had come across the writings of the German resistance fighter Dietrich Bonhoeffer, someone with an unequalled talent for defending a cause to the end, highly disciplined and radical: "Freedom only exists in action." Roy promptly repaired to Germany to study him at closer quarters. The first girl he met in Göttingen was the daughter of Bethge, the friend and biographer of his idol Bonhoeffer. He married her, although at times he could not tell whether he had married her for herself or for his conversations with her father. But he did not waste too much time thinking about that. He noted the fact, and polished his motorbike. Roy's almost naïve way of looking at things was in striking contrast to the ponderous, centuries-old thinking of Cambridge. The evenings in his company were a relief.

The Copper Kettle was filling up, the first lectures were over. He regarded the students, who constituted the majority of customers, with scepticism. He was not at all interested in any of them, since for him they were all one of a kind. They looked just like their Dutch counterparts. Argumentative, for the most part unintelligent people who trilled their little tunes like accomplished musicians. In the Netherlands that sort of thing had usually incensed him, but here it blended into the scenery and he accepted the loud-mouths as unavoidable background music. Now and then he even felt some compassion for them, as when he read noticeboards like the one above his head, in which the most fearsome subject matter was recommended for consideration. "In the series 'Science and the State', George McKinnon will tonight be examining the ethics of the research scientist, with particular reference to the usurpation of the military expert into the civil service." Usurpation. K. – he could not shake off the feelings of aggression that had taken him unawares the night before in the cinema.

All at once he felt in her grip with a force he had never known before. He was unable to resist, there was no escaping the violence of his emotions. He was distraught and it cost him enormous effort to wait for it all to subside. The immediate cause was really quite banal. The film was a sentimental story about an American family, in which the father was a professor of German literature. His son was studying archaeology, and it was his first year away from home. During a conversation beside a tennis court – and it later turned out that this was their last meeting before the father's death – the son announced that he was in love. The father, embarrassed, stood up with a laugh and quoted in a heavy American accent: "*Entweder ein schneller Tod, oder eine lange Liebe*" – either a quick death or a long love.

At that, the camera swung round to a corner of the tennis court where the son's girlfriend was picking up a ball. Under her tennis skirt you could see a pair of light blue terry-cloth knickers. And with that glimpse, the light blue panties, his longing for K. and his fear at losing her seized him uncontrollably. K., of course, had exactly the same sort of panties, which she wore at night. Over them she usually wore a threadbare T-shirt, so short that her navel was exposed. And yet it did not seem that it was this simple erotic association that had triggered the shock. There must have been something in that scene that went beyond the mere evocation of K.'s presence. He refused to accept that the quotation itself had affected him so much, though it must have somehow influenced his mood. There was also a funny little reference to his own father. Just before the man had risen from the armchair and come out with the idiotic pronouncement, he had clapped his hand on the young man's shoulder, leaned back a little, lifted his feet and then, in a rolling motion, risen to his feet. It was a perfect imitation of his own father. Not a detail he could associate with K.

The coming and going all around him did not distract him. He sat there, all his concentration focused on K., despairing of her absence, despairing of her inscrutability, despairing of her unsettled state, more than ever convinced that life without her could hardly be borne. K. had come to inhabit every nook and cranny of his mind. A masquerade, smokescreens of words, enthusiasms, theories, books, the poetic rejection of reality – his life joined seamlessly with Cambridge. The contrast with K.'s completely defenceless ways was clear-cut. She left herself exposed, asked for nothing, did nothing, and allowed the solitude to wash over her. Helpless, tormented, frightened, anxious, sometimes the resistance crumbled. A vanishing speck in the terror of infinite space: K. understood the phrase better than he did. He did not dare to face the final emptiness, but she did. That was another reason why he had decided to leave the Netherlands; his post-doctoral studies had been an excuse. What good was philosophy and literature if he could not hang on to K. and her desolation even for a year? He was making too much of it. K. had not wanted to tie him down. She kept him at arm's length as best she could, refusing to surrender to anything or to anyone. But she was also attracted by his unrelenting attention; at times she was captivated by his boyish ability to be nice to her. He was able to lift her to unsuspected heights of light-heartedness that he alone, she did not know how, could wring from her. A relationship grew that was almost aimless, changing from day to day, developing at random. He trampled through her world in clodhopping boots, sure all the while that he was in stockinged feet. What he said and did had some truth in it, but he seldom appreciated that it was better to keep silent.

He looked at his watch, pushed the little table to one side and left the café. The small centre of Cambridge was filled with people and cars. He navigated his way through the crowd. Down Trinity Street and past the Blue Boar, where he occasionally took tea in the afternoon while ploughing through the *Collected Poems* of T. S. Eliot. Clowning that appealed to him. The Blue Boar, where Bloomsbury had called and top spies such as Burgess and Philby had eaten cake. Nabokov had sat there after his exams, and Bertrand Russell. He could produce whole lists of names, each with a brilliant career – he enjoyed amusing himself with his capacity to identify with other times. Surface nostalgia, literary nonsense.

He deliberately took a different way back to the College. Through St John's Street and Bridge Street to Magdalene Street, where there was a small shop selling trinkets near the bridge. Two men and a woman sat there at a workbench making rings and bracelets with small files and chisels. He was looking in from the street at a silver necklace that had been lying in the window for several days. He wanted to buy it for K. but for one reason or another he could never make up his mind to walk into the shop. K. had no particular liking for jewellery. She never wore bracelets or rings. But this was different, he considered the necklace more than a beautiful design. This time he did not hesitate, he bought it and walked on along Magdalene Street. It was a relief that the necklace had still been there. He had the feeling that he was performing a symbolic act. Until then he never dared give K. anything; they avoided gestures with even the shadow of a definite commitment. Giving was something shameless, an encroachment on a silent understanding. Buying her a necklace was an extremely intimate act.

He remembered that after the accident that had killed her husband she had to wear a plaster collar for weeks. She briskly cast it off one day, pieces of it flying through the room. He was stupid enough to worry about her health. Silver for plaster, was that his answer? In that case, she would lay the thing to one side and forget all about it. No, it was more primitive than that, the simple belief that if she accepted his necklace she would no longer be able to vanish from his life. The motives of an insecure character, symbolic of a weakness, a form of low-level exorcism.

———

He left Cambridge, but Cambridge never left him. With K., he lived in a desultory way. They kept a cautious eye on each other. Drifting along.

On the way to his house in The Hague, where he had not been for almost a week, he drove soundlessly through the dead streets of the Indonesian district. Malakka, Bali, Lombok, Riouw.

Slowly he went inside. It was cold. He stopped in the middle of the living room and looked out. Everything had its own irrefutable space. The coach house in which he lived was surrounded by shrubs and trees. Ivy grew right up to the back door. Stumps of old rambler roses stuck out of the ground. A rusted basin lay half-buried in the soil at the edge of the terrace. Birds were flicking up the leaves. It was growing dark. He could hear the refrigerator in the kitchen starting up with a brief clunking noise. The small painting he had put up a week earlier had slipped, string hanging below it. The new lamp stood exactly where his father had put it, white tape wound around the lead. "First a cup of coffee, boys, I'm tired," his father had said when he had driven up the narrow track to the coach house and carried the lamp from the car. "A little lamp for your desk." All his movements had been sluggish. His face had been held together by shadows and lines. But there was nothing to warn him that death was so close that he would die the following night.

When saying goodbye at the corner of the house where the car was parked, he had nearly forgotten that he never kissed his father any more. He had bent over to kiss his cheek, until he realised what he wanted to do. He had stopped, halfway, a moment of confusion. Then he had shaken his father's hand, standing close to him.

In the darkened room he continued to think steadily of his father. A disciplined stream of memories, a clean wound. He pushed the chair up to his desk and started to write. Doors flung open inside him. He wrote without a break until late into the night.

———

Even as he climbed into the far too large Cadillac – and for a second had to remind himself where he was – he did not think of what he was about to do. He thought of the hundreds of times he had cycled to school from this street in which the cars were now beginning to move. It was no chance association. He had often come across funeral processions in the town. He had tried to keep up with them on his bicycle, always successfully because of their crawling speed; sometimes, at traffic lights, he manoeuvred his bike up to the front car and peered under the small light-grey curtains. As a sign of regard for the one who was lying there he had sometimes allowed himself be pulled along by the hearse, his hand clutching the broad sill. He had always counted the cars, the number of people in each of them, and studied their faces. He could also tell which private cars were part of the procession. On these occasions he had experienced a mixture of feelings: distance from what had to be taking place behind the windows and a longing for the intimacy that seemed to unite such a group of people. It had always fascinated him. He on his bicycle on the way to school, through Groenendaal, Oostplein, Blaak, Witte de With, Mathenesserlaan, Wytemaweg, with more than a hundred test papers in his bag, and they with a body on the way to Zuid or Boezemsingel. From very early on he grasped and appreciated the bizarre contrast. He had no morbid preoccupations, no more so than most people at any rate, but the intensity with which he had watched the black line of motorcars was probably somewhat unusual for someone his age. Still, he had never really believed that one day he, too, might take part in such a cortège. Perhaps as a kind of game, briefly imagining how he might be involved in someone's death, but never in earnest.

They drove slowly through the city, Groenendaal, Blaak, towards Zuid. Bicycles passed them. He noticed how agreeable the snail's pace felt. It was early January and the day was remarkably warm and still. The hazy blue sky reached down to the roof of the car in front. Distracted, he remembered the time his father had walked up to him in King's Parade. It had been quite unexpected. True, he was aware that his father was on a motoring holiday in England and, knowing him, he was sure that he would be taking "a quick look" at Cambridge, but it had been unexpected all the same. He watched him moving out of the way of a shopkeeper who was putting out a tray of sports goods. He was wearing his old green coat and the hat that had become a little rumpled over the years. He gave him a boyish grin, patently delighted at having taken his son by surprise, and had held out a somewhat limp hand for a moment. "Bonjour!" That was the way his father would greet him in the most unlikely places in the world, as if he just happened to be in the neighbourhood. With a few words, he steered his father into an antique shop close to the Fitzwilliam Museum. The owner was an expert on boxes that, on closer inspection, turned out to be writing cases. Despite the bright autumn weather, the lights in the shop, which lay below street level, were on. The sun did not reach the basements here, and the antiques were dotted about in the semi-darkness. The place resembled a deluxe vault. The small boxes were of flawless mahogany or ebony. When the lids were opened, a lean-to stand was lifted into a slanting position, revealing inkwells and writing materials under-neath let into the wood. They were travelling cases, which officers and merchants had used to write their letters in centuries past. His father inspected them thoroughly, checking the locks and handles and looking for marks of restoration and woodworm. Some of them still contained old letters and accounts. Then he said, "I sometimes dream of going on a long journey all round the world, of the time when you could carry a case like that in your luggage." He bought one of the most handsome and least ornate examples on the spot, fetched his car which he had left near Market Hill, and together they carried the purchase outside. They lifted it onto the back seat and stood in the street looking at it through the window. The brass work on the wooden box was gleaming.

———

Mounting the lectern took a few seconds, and then he looked down on the hundreds of people who crowded into the shell-shaped hall. He knew almost all of them. He stood in a similar hall after the death of K.'s husband. He had been asked to speak, about K., about her husband, about a brief love and a sudden death. About a friendship that had lasted for seven years. When he had finished speaking, he escorted K. past the many mourners. Somewhere in the throng, a man had shot to his feet. Diffident, dedicated, serious, he had stood there – his father. The next moment a wall of people rose. The noise they had made, the rustling clothes, the brief scraping of chairs and shoes, had burst like a storm over them. Everything else had been completely silent. He had been convinced he would have to lie flat on the ground in order not to be swept away.

Briefly, he reviewed his father's life. The evening before he had cooped himself up in his coach house, feeling as if he were sitting in a theatre, or in a cinema. Impressions of his father, real impressions, had flashed before him, and he had written them down one by one. He had left the curtains open. The garden and the rest of the house were in darkness. Only the lamp on his desk was lit.

He had drawn on the limits of his powers, without effort or inhibition. There had been no reservations, no place

47

where he could escape from the loss. His father's death had absorbed him completely. It was like his love for K. Later he would sometimes be unable to distinguish between the loss of his father and his love for K.

He spoke, and in the clear concentration of the moment he noted the minutest details of the people who were listening to him. The tip of a handkerchief protruding from a pocket, the sleeve of an umbrella drooping over a leg. He caught sight of people he had not seen for a long time. He saw K. sitting there, her white face turned towards him, motionless and compassionate. He nodded to her briefly, as if that was what was expected. For a moment he thought he saw his father, towards the back between a couple of his colleagues from the office – a banal impression he could not suppress.

He eventually fell silent, and heard the stillness that had now stolen over everyone there. As he walked out of the hall, the hundreds present rose as one. He knew that would happen. There was a burst of subdued noise. He looked, but this time it was not his father who had prompted the memorial salute.

"PLEASE COME IN," THE MAN WHO OPENED THE door said to him, "I am the First Secretary" – the r's rolled like breakers through his English, and the light gleamed on his shiny East-European jacket. He went into the embassy, where the Hague cultural crowd was already milling around the buffet. He had come here to meet Ellen, who would introduce him to the Hungarian ambassadress. Ellen, who had fallen upon him like a leech since he had written a few nice things about Hungary in a newspaper. Ellen, who had foisted a conference on him, an international conference for academics, artists and journalists. He belonged to none of these groups except in an oblique way. He really belonged nowhere. He was waiting for something, collecting impressions for later. An altogether indefinable, incomprehensible and insubstantial "later". Sometimes he thought that his world already lay behind him.

The place felt uncomfortably crowded, with everyone talking at the tops of their voices. It was lucky that he knew nobody. Then he spotted the woman who had brought him here and at the same moment she called out: "Quiet please, everybody, the Szëbö ensemble from Budapest will shortly play."

People began to throng into the room, holding their glasses and canapés. He, on the contrary, walked against the stream into an adjoining empty hallway. From there he watched three young men in jeans and loose shirts making ready their instruments. The deserted little room was dark, the corner where the ensemble took up their positions almost too brightly lit. He watched as a girl walked up to the young men with cautious steps and a controlled body.

She turned to face the audience and in measured tones the musicians started to play. She looked nowhere, at nobody. But she abruptly started dancing, her movements as impassive as her expression. The music behind her broke away from the leisurely pace of the beginning. Her feet tapped, she yielded to the rhythm, but it was as if it were all taking place beyond her. He could not take his eyes off her. The unresisting movements, her cool demeanour in the midst of the commotion she herself was creating – the contrast was palpable. He hoped she would never stop, unless it was to leave with him. One of the musicians put down his violin, took her by the waist and swung her around. She let him, twirling more and more rapidly.

The music came to a dead stop, and the girl stood stock-still, not caught off balance even for a second. She gave a shy smile. The audience applauded loudly, too loudly for his liking, and began to circulate again. The girl became caught up in the group of violinists. Ellen gave her a quick embrace.

What he had seen had deeply branded him.

———

In the aeroplane taxiing down the runway everything rattled. Creaking in all its joints, the machine left the concrete and crept up to the required height.

He was on his way to Hungary with Ellen and feeling very sceptical about the whole enterprise. Poets, academics, newspapermen, where did he fit in?

It was growing dark when they landed at Budapest airport. Briskly his guide shepherded him through customs. An interpreter from the conference had come to fetch them, and Ellen, Hungarian by birth, set to work on him. He was unable to make out a single sound of the disjointed language, had not a word to go by. A taxi stood waiting and its door slammed shut right across their conversation. Budapest, suburban streets at first, and then with ever-increasing speed into the centre. A death-defying drive. The driver appeared to be a boxer snatched out of the ring, now busily setting about his fellow drivers. He didn't really care. All he wanted to know was whether he would see the girl from the embassy again. Hungary meant little to him, he knew neither the country nor the language, and it was only the name of Budapest itself that rang a bell. He had once met a boy who had been in the uprising. A small boy, twelve years old, just as he was at the time, who had kept guard with a pistol in his hand – it could hardly have been more romantic. A boy with a loaded pistol and a girl who had danced in a mansion in The Hague, that was all that Budapest meant to him.

———

People had recommended the Hungaria to him, the most gilded and venerable restaurant in the city. The days of the Austro-Hungarian monarchy still made themselves felt, sixty years on. Some things refuse to vanish, no matter how much time has gone by. Though his father had died years before, his life seemed to go on and on.

The waiters gathered wordlessly around his table, a superabundance of service. One handed him a bulky menu. He could not make up his mind and kept roving back and forth between the pages. Of all the times he had eaten out with his father, he was reminded in particular of the evening when they had come back from Friesland and had put up at an old-fashioned hotel in Ommen. They sat waiting underneath an enormous painting of a meadow with cows. A thick fog had hung over the River Vecht and candles were lit on all the tables. The small dining room was empty except for a single waiter folding napkins. His father had pushed his chair back and walked to the window overlooking the river. Hands in his pockets, he nodded towards the view and said, "Weather for mah-jong."

He came up to join him and answered, "No, bezique."

His father laughed and leant his forehead gently against

52

the window, a little steamed up from the warmth inside. On the terrace the fog had swirled around the bright lights. They had stood like that hundreds of times at home with their hands on the radiators, looking out as the homing pigeons of the man across the street skimmed in wide circles over the roofs. Mah-jong, bezique – these words were primitive sounds for him and probably for his father as well. The arrival of the first course interrupted their game. His father tapped him on the shoulder: "Dinner's ready."

The waiters turned away with the order he had been obliged to give them in the end. He had been in Budapest three days now and fitted into the place with unexpected ease. It was early October, the end of summer that year, with blue skies, the trees in full colour and the light filtering through a hint of mist. He played truant from the conference as often as he could. He had come to know a few people during his short stay here with whom he took a meal or had a drink in the Café Vörösmarty, and he walked tirelessly through the town, a town that seemed to him genial beyond his comprehension.

"You don't know what freedom is. You don't know its limits, there is nothing to hold you back. You live in a dump called freedom."

He heard the pathos in the sentences, but he also heard their meaning. That afternoon he and other conference delegates were invited to attend a youth group, where they were asked to speak about the West. The hall was packed.

Pleasant faces, friendly words. Until he had asked tactlessly if they had read Solzhenitsyn, and if not why not. A deathly hush had fallen. The embarrassment he had caused rebounded on him. Then a young man got up to speak.

"We live here, it's our country, and we love it. We have a brother country. You can choose your friends but not your brothers."

And the young man carried on speaking, about his ideas and motives. And in all his words a yearning resounded, an inexpressible longing for something that had once been or might still come.

The grandiose lobby of the Hungaria loomed over him like a cathedral. He was in a sumptuous catacomb. Marble from top to bottom, mirrors and gilded wall lights, and high above him gleaming balustrades. The place was never completely filled, not even with sound. People sat about here and there, but if anything they confirmed the sense of desolation. He thought of the girl from the Szëbö ensemble; he had been thinking of her ever since he had been driven into Budapest. He could not have said why, she had not even been out of the ordinary. She had danced, and her face and far-away expression had touched him. Emotions from out of the blue. It was happening more and more often that for no apparent reason he would feel a pang on seeing a young woman's face. He had not dared to speak to her, she had been so reticent and unassuming, except when she danced. He had caught a glimpse of her looking into a mirror, and – suddenly conscious of herself –

running her hands through her hair. He would have to ask Ellen whether the girl lived in the city. He would like to see her if he could.

———

A hullabaloo of people, French, Cuban, Vietnamese, a bag of countries shaken out into the Academy of Sciences in Országház Street. He was sitting at the back of a hall wearing headphones and waiting for the end of a lecture. It was utter nonsense, a concatenation of clichés spoken in tones that seemed to be typical of the grandchildren of the revolution. Clichés, terror, dictatorship – to his father, Eastern Europe had not been much of a threat; he had never been afraid of Communists, but he had been unable to tolerate their lies.

He put his earphones down discreetly and walked to the broad balcony overlooking a walled garden. Through the open doors he saw Ellen in conversation with a heavily-built Romanian, a man he had noticed on the official platform and immediately put down as a government agent. How many of those present had links with some intelligence service? Would he himself be placed on a list because he had been invited to a contaminated country? Probably. The Hungarian embassy, Budapest – it was not impossible that the enemy might have made overtures to him. His friend Steven worked for the Dutch secret service, analysis section. He had occasionally reproached him on that account. Had thought it an unreal world, with sinister players who never knew what they knew and never understood what they understood, because everything was said to fit into some greater whole. A greater whole they did not see, but in which they nonetheless believed.

Steven defended the game. Once you had accepted that there were power blocks which wanted to know what the others were up to, then the road was open to joining a whole range of secret services. And that meant accepting a complicated system of rules. Reality? Who could claim to fathom that, who decided which were phantoms and which were not? In the secret service you soon realised that there was no reality. From its vantage point you could clearly see that reality was an arbitrary collection of odds and ends. No-one understood anything, no-one. Even the smallest fragment of your existence refused to fit into a greater whole. There was no greater whole, the very idea that there was one was a chimera. In the intelligence service people worked strictly on their own; they had no links with anyone else, which was all for the best. Steven's arguments were often logical and intelligent, and yet something was lacking in them. The hope he had always entertained was that there were ineluctable connections in his life and that he would discover them one day. A vague hope that, one way or another, some traces of a plan would be revealed. But he himself relied on nothing but old trails, a wilderness of memories. Budapest was a setting for memories in which he kept meeting his father. His father was the constant factor, recollections of him the only links between an accumulation of dreams and thoughts. Without the death of his father, nothing seemed to stay.

"I looked all over for you yesterday! Where were you?" Ellen bore down on him as he crossed the balcony.

"In the Hungaria. In your own bourgeois past," he said, more light-heartedly than he had intended. He had more or less avoided her since she had danced too close to him on the hotel dance floor.

"Do you know who I ran into in the metro, of all people? Vera, that girl from the Szëbö ensemble you were so keen on seeing again. She gave me her telephone number."

He remembered mentioning the girl to Ellen in the aeroplane. He took the slip of paper with a number on it.

"And I've also been able to fix up the interview for you with the Minister of Culture. That's what you wanted, wasn't it?"

She was quite irrepressible, an indefatigable gypsy of a woman. He thanked her and decided to go into the city. He took the shortest route to the Danube, crossed Erzsébet Bridge and climbed quickly up to an old castle, part of which had been converted into a coffee house. Outside, chairs had been placed alongside the parapet. On a diagonal below him the river ran peacefully, soaking up the noise of the streets and the quaysides.

On days like this, with an October sun on the cusp between autumn and winter, the horizon never stops shifting. From the height where he had stopped to look, he could not get enough of the view. He saw and felt the past and present beginning to merge into each other. There was no future; he was the master of time.

———

Their hands shielding their eyes against the fierce sun and the sparkle of the water, they peered at the other bank. His father rang a bell in a wooden box, the kind inside which a crucifix would have been attached a little further south. They were about to cross the Waal, their Waal, where they knew all the villages on the dykes. They fished here from the groynes and swam from the small, surprisingly white beaches. His father had grown up in Gorkum; the Maas and the Waal were the Jordan in which he had baptised his children. In the distance lay the Van Lookeren brickworks. The ferry put out from the quay, and an arm waved behind the window of the wheelhouse. In five minutes it would be there. He glanced to the side. His father's face had grown old, battered by his unyielding illness. Smoke from his cigarette coiled between them.

"Let's go to Loevestein again. The tourists have all left, it's lovely there now."

His father nodded. The river was running high. The ferry which had picked them up was swept along by the current and they had made in a wide arc for the landing stage. Then they drove across the dyke past Brakel towards Loevestein. The cattle were in the fields still. Tethered goats paced their laps next to the overgrown winter dyke. From time to time farmers lifted a slow arm to them. He knew the road like the back of his hand. Straight across the fields on a sandy track full of enormous potholes that gradually gave way to asphalt. All the way along both sides were little streams covered with water-lily pads. Horses cantered alongside the car, brought to a halt at the end of their field. Close to the castle, a rusted single-track railway line ran across the road. And then, inside a broad circle of poplars and beeches, there was Loevestein. Within its walls, the little street with the half-restored houses lay very still. Their footsteps echoed. There was no-one about; not even the warden emerged. A mulberry tree, with fruit that spurted blood when you squeezed it, marked the place where he wanted to take his father: a tower, away from the main building, with an unobstructed view of the river. They climbed up as far as a ladder leading to a trap door that gave onto the flat zinc roof.

"You're sure it's still worth it?" his father asked.

"You'll see in a moment. Take your hat off. It's a bit of a squeeze up here."

He had opened the hatch, stepped onto the roof and given his father a hand to pull him up the last few feet.

He had heard him murmur "magnificent" just once, but for the rest they had kept silence for several minutes. The landscape strung out before them was their native soil, this was where they belonged. On either side of the river there were water meadows with their groynes pointing like index fingers into the water; the monotonous calls of a cuckoo rang out nearby. They listened to the silence between the calls, and heard ships passing each other with a short blast of their horns.

His father put his hat back on. Its brim cast a shadow over his face. Despite the light it was as if he had stepped into the dark. They could see Gorkum, Woudrichem, Brakel, Vuren, Poederooijen. A couple of gulls floated lazily by. Then his father took some old biscuits from his coat pocket and tossed them one by one straight into their beaks.

"Let's go."

———

The conference had wound up several days before. Speeches, receptions, dinners. Mátyá's Pince, Fekete Holló, Bajkél – all the unpronounceable names of the cafés where they had sat deep into the night. He guessed that the small group he had hung around with was the only one that had refused to be taken in. An Englishman, an East German, a Hungarian and two Dutchmen. It was chiefly the East German who galvanised their conversations. An unobtrusive man, but unequivocal in his opinions. Someone who had decided at the age of fifty-five no longer to beat about the bush and to speak his mind. He would no more be cowed, which, incidentally, did not mean that he had chosen the West, but that he wanted a different East. This man made him feel more uncertain than he cared to admit even to himself. He admired the man's intransigence, noted how he set his past to one side and forged ahead with all guns blazing. One afternoon, when they were having tea in a pavement café on Kossuth Square, he said: "Don't forget that there could come a moment in your life when you must turn your back on all your freedom in order to make a choice. And if that moment doesn't come, you won't need to die any longer, you'll be dead enough already."

The sermon of a Communist? Freedom, action, death – in what kind of categories did these people think? As the traffic sped by them and he watched the pigeons scratching about between the parked cars, he reflected how remote his life was from the kind of life this German was describing. A life without excuses, without melancholy, without a cherished past.

The others at the table had fallen silent too.

The delegates to the conference had dispersed, and he alone stayed on in the city. Ellen had given him a handful of pieces of paper containing addresses. Budapest looked more beautiful than ever. The Indian summer continued and he roamed the city centre following a well-worn beat. For longer distances he took the tram.

As he did on the evening when he decided to go to the circus. It was dusk. He climbed onto the tram, and everything he saw and touched seemed utterly familiar. There were few other passengers, the woman driver in the front being separated from them by a curtain. It was an exact replica of the trams in which he had sometimes ridden to school. The bare lights on the walls, the worn black leather benches – the tram journey eased him back into his earliest years: streets with shops, a vegetable auction, a small market where people were still hastily buying things from the half-dismantled stalls. Twilight, colourless terraced houses, open windows with women leaning out to gossip with their neighbours. Enduring, timeless, gone by before it could be taken in, a small cosmos of gestures. It flashed vividly out of sight and left you alone.

He rode on to the terminus, got out and found himself in the yard of a depot. With dimmed lights the deserted tram awaited its return journey. The conductor gave him directions to the circus and he set off, the long road before him unexpectedly making him feel that he was alone in a strange town. The suburb where he had ended up seemed wholly cut off from the life of the city. The pleasing sensation generated by the rocking tram was gone. Gloomy houses alternated with shuttered shops and small factories. Across the street he made out the illuminated entrance to a hospital.

He walked slowly on, the events of that afternoon crowding in on him with an irresistible force.

At two o'clock he had taken a taxi to the Ministry of Culture, where he was to interview the minister. He walked into the building, and while looking for someone to show him the way, kept turning into passages that led nowhere. He found it strange that there was no doorman to usher him in. He had still not made any progress when a woman in a grey suit came towards him, took charge, and opened a door. She was, it appeared, his assigned interpreter.

A man stepped forward from behind his desk, a bare desk in an almost bare barn of a room. The leather sofas on which they sat down looked to him like samples from a furniture store.

"A trial has just started in Prague of members of Charter '77. What is your view of that?"

He had intended to lead up to the question gradually, but instead posed it straight away, almost afraid of forgetting it. The Hungarian gave him a friendly but noncommittal look.

"Where did you get that story? I know nothing about it."

"From yesterday's *Herald Tribune*."

Usually, he bought the *Herald Tribune* in the Astoria, where he went for coffee every morning. The Astoria was a hub of non-Communist activity. Black marketeers, prostitutes, money changers, rich Arab businessmen – it was an interesting hotel.

"Oh, well, the *Herald Tribune*. And you believe them! I think they've got hold of the wrong end of the stick. But if there *is* a trial going on, that's the Czechs' business, we have nothing to do with it."

He thought how incensed his father would have been at this evasion.

"Amnesty International estimates that there are 200 political prisoners in your country. What is your answer to that?"

The minister was about to reply when a thunderous clatter filled the room. Outside the open window a man

63

stood drilling holes in the asphalt, making machine-gun sounds. The minister rose and closed the window, but the racket hardly diminished. Walking back to his chair he came out with the stock answer, "In Hungary, there are no political . . ."

All at once he lost any desire to hear another word, his concentration shifting to an evening buried deep in his consciousness which he rarely allowed to the surface. It was no doubt because of the deafening drill, and the minister, who kept talking and talking.

The telephone rang. "For you," someone called out above the repetitive but insistent music from "Butch Cassidy and the Sundance Kid". "It's for you."

He picked up the receiver, pressing a palm against his other ear. He heard a woman's voice.

"Thank goodness I've managed to find you. I couldn't get you at home. Your father's been taken to hospital, he wants you to come. Go straight to the Harbour Hospital, it looks quite serious to me."

Someone offered him a glass of beer with a smile, knowing that he had no free hands. He grinned back, shook his head, and realised that he was a hundred kilometres from his father's home.

"What's happened? Is he dead?"

"No, no, I don't know exactly what's wrong. An ambulance came for him half an hour ago. On the stairs he told me to ring you. He was on a stretcher and he seemed calm."

Within a minute he was in his car. It was cold. Pockets of long-standing snow spotted Austerlitz Forest as he raced through it. The exhaust fumes had floated like large white butterflies in his wake. His whole body was thudding. He spoke aloud to his father, hammered his hands on the steering wheel, banged his fist against the dashboard and said the same phrase over and over throughout the drive: "Hold on, hold on!" And underneath, on the calm surface of his intuition, the words: he is dead, he is dead, ticked away with utter certitude. Austerlitz to Rotterdam, a death-defying drive. A drive against time, an impossibility. He rounded Oostplein as the Harbour Hospital loomed up through the evening mist. He had been here dozens of times to visit his father, a regular customer. He flung the door of his car open, ran to the main entrance, and the first person he saw was his brother, who took a few steps towards him holding his hands up in despair. He saw the tears on his face, saw the brightly-lit entrance hall with its flower stall closed. He saw his mother, still and pale. She led him to a small room just beyond the entrance. A nurse said, "Please come in." There his father lay, still and pale like his mother. He placed a hand on his forehead. It felt cold, unnervingly cold. The face above the sheet looked apologetic. Because he had been unable to ward off death, because he could not talk any more, because his hands . . . The nurse had asked them to leave. Strange rules, they had only just come, and whom could they be disturbing?

In the afternoon his father had suddenly felt warm, terribly warm, his mother told him. This was the litany, the lament, the last day, the last hour, the last moment. He went for a walk to shake off the warmth. He was on the verge of letting the cold in for good. At dinner he had not said much. The warmth was gone, but even so he took to his bed. And then, as if decreed from unknown regions, nausea, pain, the body resisting one more time. He asked for the doctor to come. When the men came into the bedroom with a stretcher, still he tried to help them. He got off the stretcher for a moment while they held it at an angle in order to get it through the door. His last steps. He had lifted his head up on the stairs and said that his sons would have to be warned. His last words. He was slid into the ambulance, perhaps at that point no longer alive. A male nurse had pounded his chest with his fists, pounded and pounded. Hard enough to crack his ribs. The battering of a body that had reached its limit. He listened to his mother, to the lament, the sorrowful litany, until it ebbed away. Her story told, she fell silent. He looked around the room in his parents' home and noticed that the Christmas tree was shedding its needles. A faint smell of mandarins was in the air, peel lay on the edge of his ashtray. It was December 29, a day signifying nothing, a breathing space in the calendar. Or a day on which to go no further. He lit several candles at random and said something resembling a prayer. The incantations of a rainmaker, a Jew's Kaddish, a Catholic's Latin phrases, nothing but words reaching into the dark: Father, I am here, where are you?

The minister was non-committal. The uninterrupted noise and clatter had put him in a state of lucid alertness. The film of his father's death was running inside his head even as he faced the minister and continued with mounting anger to question him. The visit lasted an hour, and he sat there earnestly taking notes and asking the interpreter to repeat some remark from time to time. The whole thing resembled an interview, but he knew that he would not use any of it. The man would not be drawn, he piled phrase upon phrase. When eventually he left the ministry, he noticed that the road in front of the building was one big hole.

The evening in this remote district was extraordinarily dark. Walking down the deserted streets, he lost all sense of direction. The meeting with the minister, the anniversary of his father's death, disoriented him. He stopped for a moment and saw a car brake at an angle behind him, in front of the hospital entrance. Someone went inside unhurriedly; he could follow his progress for a while through the glass doors. At last the circus he was making for came into sight, but he forced himself to keep walking. For the first time he longed to be at home. When he reached the circus building, he decided to ring Vera, no longer in the mood to mess about with tigers and lady acrobats. The next morning he would fly back to Amsterdam, and he hesitated until the last moment whether to approach the girl from the embassy. He dialled the number and a voice said something incomprehensible. He gave his name. It was Vera. Yes, she had heard about him and would be pleased to meet him. "I'm rehearsing tonight with a dance group in the high school in Kondor Street, the Gymnasium, can you find that?"

He would be there. Her voice had sounded friendly; he had supplied the missing words in her English from time to time. It was half past eight, and he had arranged to meet her at ten. The foyer from which he had telephoned was empty. A few latecomers dashed past him up the stairs. The performance must have started, for he heard a muffled flourish of trumpets.

He took a street leading downhill. He had not noticed that the circus was on a hill on the way there. The sky was black and starless, and there was no wind. It seemed that few people lived in this neighbourhood, and the poor lighting lent everything a lack of definition. He had to take care not to trip over places in the street that had been dug up. He took hold of an iron railing along one side. Beyond it the slope rose to a point he could not see. Shrubs formed an untidy border. He reached a path leading down from the street level to a wooden-built restaurant with an advertisement for a local brand of beer above the door, brightly lit by a small spotlight. He was hungry and went in. A bare room with a few chairs at some already-laid tables on a platform. He took a chair and sat, waiting motionless for someone to serve him. His journey was over. Budapest had become like his hometown. One day he would surely return in an attempt to relive it all. His passion for the past also governed his future. He would have to introduce changes there; he could not continue to draw his life out in front of him and look backwards at how it had been.

He scrutinised the man who emerged from the kitchen. A Hungarian he would never see again, a stranger who stood in the limelight for a moment and would melt into the shadows again. People were part of the world's stage; they were there, but you did not know them. They existed, but outside you, with no lasting form or size. It was all one great shadow play lit up by the sun and the moon. Phantoms, a Wajang show. Tomorrow he would be going home, his head filled with emotions.

———

The stewardess on the Malev airliner gave him a nod. He took that to be encouraging. It was the same kind of propeller aircraft he had flown on coming in, although if possible yet more dilapidated. But it flew. He had looked up Vera, Vera whom he had seen dancing months before. It was one of the thousands of scenes that land on one's retina and disappear from it sooner or later, no matter how strong an impression they make. But like someone who cannot cope with his loss, so irrationally he wanted to recapture the old feeling. He took a taxi to Kondor Street. The driver had not known exactly where the gymnasium was and dropped him halfway up the street. It was not long before he caught sight of a building that could be nothing other than a school. It seemed ironic that an institution like a classical high school should have existed in a socialist country. The vast quantities of elitist material digested there had become suspect even in his own country. But there was no doubt the gymnasium existed, and its staircases were redolent of that unmistakable smell of school. There were no lights on anywhere, and all that guided him was a small red illuminated sign saying "Exit" – the Latin word, a clear indication that he had come to the right place. As hopelessly as he had lost his way in the Ministry of Culture, here he unerringly found his way through the school. He opened a door to a classroom bathed in pink and blue light like an aquarium. Boys and girls sat on the desks listening to pop music. Somebody called out to him. As he continued upstairs he could hear the tapping of feet on a wooden floor. The stairs led to a short passage. He saw a sports hall, neon-lit, wall bars, ladders, rings and springboards. He stopped in shadow in the passage, where the light from the hall could not reach him. And there, among the dozens of dancers, he saw her. She was dancing. She was dancing as she had done in the embassy, but this time without musical accompaniment. Her legs were bare and she wore a ballet costume with wide sleeves. He thought her beautiful, more beautiful than he remembered. As he looked at her, he felt again that nameless sorrow. She was untouched by the cold light of the neon. She seemed to be drawing back from herself, moving almost with languor, but with no vestige of self-consciousness. And he, in the darkness of the passage, slowly raised his hand and waved. She did not see him. He turned around, closed his eyes for a second and walked away.

Backwards.

"YOU'LL BE ABLE TO TELL YOUR FRIENDS THAT you saw Lester Piggott ride in a race," Willems said to him as the shouting around them grew louder.

"No-one in the Netherlands knows who Piggott is and if you don't point him out I won't know myself," he replied, his voice croaking.

The racecourse formed a large oval loop laid in the English countryside. Even from a distance, everything suggested hallowed ground. Roads approached cautiously from various directions, but nowhere did the traffic encroach upon a domain in which horses took pride of place.

Goodwood in Sussex. The Dukes of Richmond had been living here since time immemorial, which meant several centuries. He had never watched a race from so close and his excitement was all the greater for it. Willems and he were in the grandstand, surrounded by a nonchalant crowd of men and women. An agile little fellow was signalling the latest odds with clown-like hands to a colleague further along. With every new race, the throng moved forward as one to the side of the track, and the shouting started – the horses' names, the jockeys' names. The subdued thudding of the hooves, the fierce snorting, would rise to a crescendo. He joined in the shouting, without inhibition, eyes fixed on his fancy of the moment. There was much pushing and pulling, flourishing of whips, and spitting and cursing. The horses were sweating, with foam on their flanks, their knees bandaged. The finishing line put an abrupt end to their headlong speed.

Willems looked at him. His normally red cheeks were almost blue. "Lost."

———

He walked into the Park House Hotel, his home at the time. Willems had picked him up in the Austin and brought him back. For no reason he could think of, he had taken a liking to the man. A somewhat rugged gentleman farmer from southern England, who laughed too loudly, flailed his arms too much and disguised his feelings. He drove like a blacksmith, accelerating at every crossing instead of braking. A creature bursting with vitality.

The door with the round handle closed behind him. Park House, Bepton. He knew this Edwardian country house down to its last detail. "Details are the nerve conduits of the truth. Describe the house, describe the plants, describe the birds. Don't just say, 'there's a bird flying past', learn its name, its call, its colour, learn to distinguish – that is the first law of good writing." Ione O'Brien was relating how a famous English author had held forth on the subject for nights on end. She was the owner of the hotel and it was one of the few times he had heard her talk about one of her guests.

It was seven in the evening. All the guests were gathering in the bar, where the walls were covered from floor to ceiling with photographs. A lifetime in frames. Photographs of guests and family. India, Churchill, Prince Charles, Ione's husband "the Major", cricket teams, polo players: the British Empire pickled in black and white.

"Brilliant article in the *Spectator* this week in favour of extending our nuclear fleet" – the sentence poised in the air like a hummingbird.

"Until the plumber gets round to repairing our drains, I don't think I'm in favour," said the hostess. The small room was filling up. Everyone was introduced to everyone else, newcomers finding themselves accepted into an instantly created family. Ione was seventy-five. Broad, plump, wearing clothes from years long past and lipstick not always exactly where it was meant to be. She cooked with a glass of whisky in her left hand, artfully weaving people together. Her thick, gnarled fingers had undergone conservatory training once upon a time. But back from India after independence, and married to a man who drew an Indian Army pension, she had bought Park House. "We had to do something, we had no money, no job, so we borrowed from my father and started the hotel." Voices with exotic accents mingled: each year different voices, different faces, different friends-for-a-few-days. Wherever

74

Ione appeared, in the dining room, in the drawing room, on the verandah with tea and cake, the habitual aversion to making contacts with strangers evaporated. The smell of the furniture, the soft red walls, the antique dinner tables, the journals in the drawing room, the tennis rackets in the hall – there was an indefinable sense of homecoming.

For fifteen years he had been coming here, in all seasons. His usual room was at the top of the house.

After drinks and before dinner, he would sit for a little while at his window. The late summer lingered in the garden; the sun had dipped behind the hills. Directly below him were two grass tennis courts surrounded by netting rather than hedges. Rosebeds bordered a croquet lawn, where pegs and hoops summoned memories of a distant youth. Hotel and garden were hemmed in by fields of wheat and corn. Gardeners had perfected the lawn over generations. The silence was underlined by the inaudible flight of a buzzard above the fields. He watched the progress of the bird of prey from tree to tree, a dark shape against a deep blue sky. Between late afternoon and evening, the most uncommitted moment of the day, poised between resignation and alienation, light and dark.

His father had stayed at Park House during the last summer of his life. Ione and his father had taken to each other immediately, she told him years later.

Speedy integration into English country life: wearing long white tennis trousers his father had joined the Major in organising tournaments for the guests. "Okker", the Major had called him, or "the Dutchman". Willems had been there too, but he had an English wife, so he no longer counted as a Dutchman. Those not playing sat on benches alongside the white chalked lines of the court. The Major urged the players on as they strained every nerve to impress the spectators. White hats, walking sticks, whispered conversations and the muted plop of the tennis ball. The drone of a harvester was heard in the distance as the sun climbed to its zenith behind the South Downs. High summer, the whole world compressed into a little under an hour of tennis on a grass court in southern England. His father laughed, wiped his forehead with a handkerchief and returned the ball just over the net with a drop shot. "Good shot, Okker, good shot!" cried the Major, standing up and pronouncing it time for a drink. He beckoned to the Dutchman, to his father, who, scarcely able to stand, clutched the top of the net, apologised and sat down on a bench, exhausted. It was an unnatural tiredness, with the heat flooding his neck and face. He was fifty-nine. Too young to die.

———

He sat there, staring out of the window. The scenes preceding his father's death, the signs, the omens, the short, unlooked-for preliminaries – he kept reviewing them in his mind at the places where he knew his father had been. Riddles of a reality that may never have existed, had certainly never existed. Snatches of memories, pointless dreams. Downstairs a door opened and one of the guests sauntered with a golf club to an immaculately cut lawn to practise his putting. After a little while he heard the soft clunk of a golf ball in the hole. He knew the game, enjoyed it, but hated the paraphenalia that went with it. He had played golf in the past at a course in the dunes at Noordwijk aan Zee. And once, during a round, he had looked up to see his father walking towards him. He could scarcely believe his eyes. Plum across the middle of the huge course, his hand clasping his hat, his father came to see how his son was doing. He marched straight across the fairways, straight through all the conventions, disappearing at times behind a dune, to emerge again through the gorse. He himself was standing on top of one of the highest dunes, and could watch his father as he went up and down hill. He watched him coming ever closer, a man unaware that he was riding roughshod over precious etiquette. The whole vista seemed focused on a single point: his advancing father.

"How's it going?" was all he said, when he arrived somewhat out of breath at the spot where they were about to tee off. The other players looked at him with irritation and disbelief.

"Seems like a good game," he added.

After that he played no more good shots. His father noticed, touched his shoulder, said, "Let me know when things improve," and retreated the way he had come. Across the dunes, straight over the fairways. It started to rain and he opened an umbrella. Then he vanished from sight; for a moment hat and umbrella stuck out above some bushes and then were gone. It was at that point that he realised how lonely his father had looked. Lonely? His father lonely? The impossible thought took hold, and his father's life gained colour as a result. Loneliness is the inseparable shadow of happiness. It was reflected in the stubbornness in his eyes, the embarrassed smile when he left. He recognised that expression, it was also there when he visited his father in hospital. He saw it all those times he had unexpectedly walked into the room and come upon his father in his chair, looking out, the lights not yet switched on, his head and shoulders shrouded in twilight. Loneliness, a decaying body, years of illness that had worn him out without his ever talking about it. A flaw in the metabolism was all he ever let on. Contracted during the Hunger Winter, according to his doctor. Their bathroom at home had a cupboard full of medicines, which had filled him with awe when he was a child. One of the first words he ever learned was "pharmacy". Yet he knew no-one with a greater capacity for enjoyment than his father.

———

The moon had just slipped over the Downs, lending the surrounding landscape an appearance of utter serenity. Everything looked wide open, a yawning chasm of possibilities.

There had been a pickup truck which was used for

transporting shells from the beach. Twenty boys stood or sprawled on its open back, in high spirits, some with a bottle in their hand, a crate of beer between them. There had been singing and shouting; they did not hear the breakers, did not see the moon.

The beach at Katwijk was full of holes. They planned to drive on for two kilometres to meet another group that was on its way from Noordwijk. It was nearly midnight. The warm wind was blowing hard. He was standing near the edge of the pickup, not drinking very much. When the truck swerved without warning he was pitched over the tailgate. He hung suspended over the rear wheel, arms dangling down, the back of his knees clamped in an instant to the wooden edge of the back of the truck. He hung there as the sand rasped across his hands, and the very same moment he had pulled himself up again, as if he were doing an exercise on the horizontal bar.

But he had heard the scream, he knew that someone had been flung out of the truck and must now be lying somewhere on the dark beach. He jumped down and ran. Behind him he could hear the commotion, in front of him a huddled figure took shape, twisted, doubled-up. Clothes all around his body, a torn shirt collar sticking up sideways from his neck. He knelt down beside him, gently holding him when the boy had called out twice with furious conviction: "I'm going to die!"

In the ambulance he pounded away on an oxygen pump, following the male nurse's directions. A futile exercise:

there was no reaction at all. Later in the waiting room he saw the boy's father run into the hospital entrance. Saw the man hesitate and stand still, how a doctor came up to him, how the numbness seized the father, the doctor's hand on his shoulder. He would remember above all the father.

———

Not long after this incident they stood on the Waal Dyke near Brakel. The water meadows were flooded, the water reaching up to the dyke, their dyke. The fisherman's cottage his father had bought in the fifties and in which they had spent so many unforgettably happy summers was about to disappear, the very first victim of the dyke-widening work. Back in the cottage, hands deep in their pockets, they looked across the river. In the dark grey water, planks bobbed against the dyke. Gulls, driven backwards in the high wind, tried in vain to make up lost ground. It was stormy, but not really cold.

His father talked, telling him how he had grown up along the Waal and the Maas near Gorkum. The family stories, about the large burgomaster's house in which they had lived, about how his mother had played Liszt's "Liebestraum", about how his father had piled up their best dinner service on a low table and had leapt over it with his sons. Slowly but steadily his father's past filled the room. Nothing suggested that he cherished his memories; he merely told what he still remembered, without fuss, without dramatic flourishes. Now and then he prompted him with questions or comments, for his father seldom spoke of his early days. In the thirties, the Stock Exchange crash had swallowed up his parents' capital; he had been a student and had witnessed the approach of the war.

"Six of us were living on a canal. On the big balcony looking over the water, we read in the papers about the escape of Jews from Germany. It caused us no more than vague disquiet. During my fifth year at college, my father died. All I remember is his voice bellowing my name. It echoed through the waiting house – my name. I ran upstairs to where my father was lying in bed. He looked surprised; he wasn't aware that he'd been calling me. He had just woken from a short nap. The next day he was dead. I have always wondered why he had called me that time, it sounded so urgent, there was so much strength in his voice. What had he been dreaming about, what had he been thinking of, why my name?"

"Have you ever been afraid of dying?" he asked his father. He had been wanting to ask him that ever since the boy's accident. Now, with water all around them, in the loft of their condemned cottage on the dyke, the question came easily.

"Yes, very much so. I remember feeling a kind of panic whenever I heard my mother playing the piano. At night I couldn't get to sleep, couldn't concentrate, and I'd often go into the street and stay out for hours. It came to me in snatches, that fear, nothing made it any better. But it has vanished now, gone. Dying is still a terrible thought, but

81

that terror is no longer there. That was because of the birth of you and your brother. The loose wires from which I was dangling were pulled tight. The two of you kept me in place. I became anchored between my dead father and mother and my living children."

His father fell silent and looked away. There had been no pathos in his voice. What he said sounded logical and natural. In the distance he could see a farm, and beyond that, Loevestein castle. In a remote corner of the Bommelerwaard, in the small house just out of the water's reach, they watched the storm.

———

"There is no such thing as thinking, thinking is an ideal. The fragmentation of our lives has gone so far that no amount of thinking can stop it. In the past, philosophers could still keep track of the whole business, but that was long ago. We have been chopped into little pieces, we can no longer see the horizon. Music is the last echo of religion. We are about to be eclipsed."

He had not noticed the man before. Ione had introduced him after dinner; he hadn't caught his name, but something in the man's face had attracted him. They were sitting on one of the benches beside the tennis court, coffee untouched on a table beside them. Lamplight fell in long ribbons over the grass, off into the darkness of the garden. The stranger did not mince his words and spoke half in dogmatic assertions and half in challenging questions to which he expected no reply.

"Only what has passed is real. If you walk ahead and then look back you can see your footprints and the ground they have crossed. The past is the only thing you can hold on to. Nothing happens that has not been started much earlier. Authenticity, originality, are hollow words, and progress, however much of our identity is bound up with it, means nothing. We all talk with our eyes closed. We are batteries charged by what has been handed down to us in our genes. We are impelled by what has already been decided, corrupted and damned, centuries ago. Forget reality, forget the truth in particular, and forget the future altogether. The future is death for you and for me. Looking ahead leads to one thing only: the discovery of your grave."

While the man beside him was doing his best to squeeze as many propositions as possible into the least possible number of words, he could see his father before him dressed in tails. For years his father would go to church in morning dress, to a progressive church with a solemn ritual. It was decreed that church council members should be distinguishable. He would join his father now and then walking through the town in the early morning. One Sunday his father had come back home disappointed. The sermon had been about the rich young man, and it had rankled with his father that the young man who had been so keen to follow Jesus should have been sent away sorrowful, told to sell everything he possessed. He was upset that someone should have been sent packing in that way, and could not get over the fact that Jesus had let such a fine young man go away in such distress.

"Religion tries to lull us to sleep, science tries to keep us awake and art has gone completely off the rails."

The man was dealing with the bigger picture and failed to notice that his neighbour was set dreaming by his prophecies. Gesticulating, almost angry, the man waited for a reaction, but it did not come.

What were his own most enduring memories? Snow on the school playground and waiting until you were finally allowed to leave the classroom, one by one. The class, absolutely still, a macrocosm of anticipation, the teacher's finger pointing to one child at a time. At long last it was your turn, you were allowed outside, out of the classroom, to walk up the corridor, put on your coat, open the door to the playground and plunge into the awe-inspiring freedom of the snow. With a pistol at his head, this would probably be the one memory that put all others in the shade. It would only have lasted a few minutes; after that they would play for half an hour, then go home red in the face from the snowball fight. No-one would have noticed what was going on. The class in semidarkness, about four in the afternoon, no-one allowed out as yet. He was ten years old at most. Up till then nothing had happened, barely a past, barely a future, only a thirty-foot-square view of the snow that had just fallen. War, sickness, death, love, literature, religion: they did not yet exist, there was no story up till then, up till then nothing had happened. He had still been a dreamer, believing in everything he saw and did not see.

This was the memory that kept returning, never varying in intensity. The excitement when he was let out, the snowy sky through the tall windows, the corners of the window-sills steeped in snow, the large round hanging lamps with their cold light. Nothing had a hidden meaning, or touched an emotion. Everything was simplicity itself, nothing was complex, there was no room for reflection. He had carried this with him unimpaired through the years, the perfect feeling.

The stranger stopped talking. The coffee was cold, and he wanted to go inside again.

"My apologies for my rather inadequate response," he said, "I'm afraid my thoughts were elsewhere." They strolled back and Ione steered a newcomer in the man's direction.

"Who is that?" he asked her.

"James Winter, the author. I thought the two of you had met. He trains horses as well." No, he didn't know him. Perhaps Willems did, he knew about horses. He must tell Willems again how much he had enjoyed the racing at Goodwood. He still had the thunder of hooves in his ears. A race against time, a race against memory on the back of a horse. He left the gathering behind in the sitting room and went upstairs. The light was out and he stopped in the middle of the room. Crickets were singing in the garden below, a waning tune of loss. The hills lay like a vague blur in the far distance, though a walker would take no more than half an hour to get to the ridge. Someone had told him that the Romans had built a road high up in the South Downs, two thousand years ago. Horses and slaves flogged through the countryside with whips for hundreds of miles, to build a road made of boulders. It was still there, the road. Half overgrown, full of cracks and sunken over the centuries. But it was there. His father had died like a Roman, he reflected. What had run through his mind on that last day? He had turned silently inward, on himself. He had left the house once or twice to take a walk. Underneath his ravaged skin the battle had started. He had not told anyone of his fears. He must have known.

He walked up to the window to close it. There is something spellbinding about a galloping horse racing to the finish. The moans, the creaking of leather, the ears flattened.

His father had called out the names of his sons, softly.

The uproar shortly before the end, the bellowing grand-stands.

Until it broke off.

He could hear nothing but the crickets in the garden.